RICK POWELL
MESSAGES

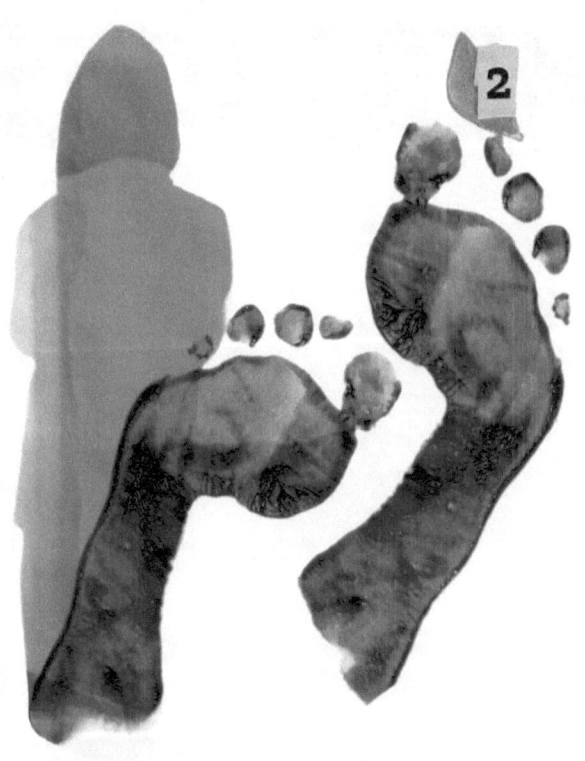

MESSAGES

RICK POWELL
WRITER

MARIE MOLDOVAN  JOE MYKUT
EDITORS

MARIE MOLDOVAN
ARTIST

Joseph Mykut -Editor

Marie Moldovan - Editor, Publication Layout, Illustration and Cover Design.

MESSAGES

I Ain't Your Marionette Press, P.O BOX 184, Larder Lake ONTARIO, P0K 1L0, Canada.

Foreword

It is with great pleasure that I introduce to you the latest masterpiece from the twisted mind of Rick Powell. Rick has once again pushed the boundaries of terror and imagination in his latest short story, "Messages."

When I first encountered Rick Powell's writing, I was immediately struck by his ability to weave intricate tales that linger long after the final page. As an illustrator, writer, and talent agent, I have the privilege of representing Rick and witnessing his journey firsthand. Our professional relationship began when I encountered his unique talent for storytelling.

Rick's journey as a writer has been one of relentless exploration into the depths of human fear and imagination. In "Messages," he masterfully blurs the lines between reality and nightmare, drawing readers into a world where the familiar becomes unsettling and the unknown lurks in every shadow.

In this chilling tale, we are taken on a journey into the heart of darkness, where the lines between reality and nightmare are blurred. Prepare yourself for a thrilling ride into the depths of horror, where the rules no longer apply, and the unknown lurks around the corner.

"Messages" is a testament to Rick's skill as a storyteller and his ability to craft tales that will taint your dreams long after you finish reading them. From mayhem to mannequins, this author flirts with the bizarre and disturbing things that haunt our darkest imaginations.

As you delve into "Messages," you will find yourself on a journey through the bizarre and the disturbing, guided by Rick's deft storytelling. His ability to evoke emotion and provoke thought is unparalleled, making this story a must-read for anyone who appreciates horror.

Enter this world of terror at your own peril, but be warned: once you begin reading, there's no turning back from what awaits you.

-Joseph Anthony Mykut
of **Cosmic Creation Station.**

Technology: A Leap Forward or an
Apocalyptic Stage?

-Pita Black

I wish it wasn't like this, you know?

Glancing at my cell phone sprawled on the tabletop in my stark apartment, I'm whisked back to a memory of when I was nine. It reminded me of a snake my sister's boyfriend had. It was so long ago, but I remember it was green and looked like a curled worm.

The snake just sat coiled on a moss-covered tree branch in his cracked aquarium. The thing that really sent a chill through me was its yellowish eyes.

They seemed frozen and alert at the same time, as if it was dreaming but conscious of everything around it in that dank, dirty basement.

Even when they fed that thing—I think it was a mouse or small rat or something—its eyes never changed.

That is how it is with my cell phone now.

Ever notice how a text, whether it's some terrible news or just a birthday shout-out, hits you with the same chill as a breeze off Lake Superior?

Doesn't matter the ringtone, could be Sinatra or a Twins of Evil soundtrack, it's all the same cold drone.

Even when you set it to vibrate or silent, it has the power to divert your attention from whatever you are doing to look at that glowing screen.

Radio back in the day? Didn't have that grip. TV? Sure, it had its moment, but now we're in the age of Wi-Fi and touchscreens. Tech's sprinting faster than a base stealer at Wrigley Field. Makes me think, when the big curtain call comes, it'll be over in a flash. Just hope I'm not around when that occurs.

***

"Hey, Jessie!"

The red-haired girl slammed both hands on the locker door in the congested hallway. Her shout muffled by the other students' voices and pounding feet rushing to various classrooms.

Jessica jumped in shock, almost dropping her cell phone as she tried to shove her overfilled backpack into her already overstuffed locker.

Dropping her backpack, Jessica yelped, "Christ, Sara! You scared the shit out of me!"

Sara giggled as Jessica picked up the backpack and once again struggled to fit it into the locker. After finally managing to do so, Jessica slammed the metal door shut with a sigh and leaned back against the locker.

Jessica swept a tangled strand of blond hair behind her ear and tapped her phone's screen, which displayed a muscular boy in a football uniform, but no new messages.

"Still no word, huh?" Sara said, her smile fading.

"No. It's been three days. I was up most of the night waiting for his text. I messaged his brother on Facebook for about an hour trying to find out what Derek had been up to, but he said, 'My bro just needs his space. The team has been working him out like crazy, finals are kicking his ass, blah, blah, blah.' I really don't need this shit now. He promised me after our fight a few days ago that he would talk to me more. I just hope that... that..." She didn't look up from her phone as she rubbed a tear from her bloodshot eye.

"Jessie, please hang in there," Sara said as she put her hand on her shoulder. "You guys have been together for two years. You know how his ego is."

Jessica remained silent, her hand, once tightly clutching her phone, now fell to her side, limp. Tearful she whispered, "I know, I know, but if he started up again talking to Lori, I don't know what I would do. You know how she got last time Derek and I fought, and I know how he looks at her sometimes, and... and..."

"Don't even think about that skank. If she pulls anything, I will kick her fucking ass and pull every goddamn blond weave off her head!" Sara said comforting Jessica with a hug.

Sara's arm remained around her friend's shoulder offering reassurance. Jessica wiped the tears from her eyes and let out a weak laugh as they both merged with the moving crowd of oblivious students.

"You have no idea how much you mean to me. I love you!" Jessica sighed as she laid her head on Sara's shoulder.

Jessica's phone vibrated, its buzz barely audible over the crowd's footsteps and chatter. Pausing, she glanced at her phone, tapping the screen to read the new message. Beside her, Sara stopped and turned to face Jessica as the stream of students flowed around them in the hallway.

"Was that Derek? What did he say?" Sara asked, her head cocked in curiosity.

Jessica looked up, her face void of emotion.

"What is wrong with your eyes?" Sara's voice quivered.

***

Jessica Sterling and Sara Rimbaud—those two lovely, bright girls. Flipping through my notes, the reports, the interviews from these past months, I'm reminded that my nightmare began with them. In this small town in the middle of Illinois, usually as peaceful as a Sunday morning on Michigan Avenue, a sudden tragedy struck.

One girl dead, the other slapped with a murder rap. It happened in an instant. Eyewitness accounts were consistent: two girls, chums, gabbing away one minute, then all hell broke loose. Next thing, one's sprawled out, and the other's gone berserk, hollering and clawing. Took a trio of linebackers to pin her down. Jessica shredded the skin off one

jock's arm like she was filleting a
perch from Lake Michigan.

The police and EMT's arrived
quickly, but it was too late. The
damage was done. The tox screens
came up clean—no dope, no horse, no
nothing. Jessica's noggin was a clean
slate, no screws loose, no demons. Now
she's holed up in a loony bin in Maine,
silent as the grave.

I still recall the faces of the
jocks I interviewed that day for the
newspaper. Their expressions
revealed a horror I had never seen
before.

I landed the job at the
Joshington County Post just three
days prior. Leaving behind the bustling
streets of Chicago, where crime rates
soared and political red tape stifled

my journalistic pursuits, I sought solace in this new town.

The daily grind—taxes, rent, the ceaseless treadmill of city life—had taken its toll. I was gunning for a little peace, maybe dodge an ulcer or an early dirt nap. I took a hit in the wallet, sure, but you can't put a price on sanity.

I had no idea moving here would be more than I bargained for.

***

"Honey, did you get that email from Sharon?" Joan called from the kitchen, the scent of the pot roast hanging in the air.

"I'll check in a bit," Alan said, clicking away on the keyboard. "I heard the renovations on their house cost them a bundle. Sharon is lucky your brother makes six figures at his law firm."

Joan appeared in the doorway of the study, untying the apron around her waist. "Do I detect a tinge of jealousy, dear? You and he were always the competitive types. Your job as a CPA is something to be proud of. We aren't exactly counting food stamps, are we?" she said with a smirk.

Alan chuckled. "Nope. I grew up with nine brothers and sisters. I know what it's like on public aid. I made damn sure I, or you, would never get to that point. Worked my ass off to get where I am today," he said, still typing and looking at the computer screen.

Joan walked up to him, leaned over, and kissed him on the cheek with a loud smack. "And I could not be more proud of you," she said, rubbing his shoulders.

She moved a stray strand of blond hair away from her face as she looked at the screen. "Honey, I told you, no working so close to dinner. Everything is ready. You know how you get caught up. Don't let dinner get cold like last time."

Alan leaned back in the chair. "Sorry, McManus forgot to include that change on his 1040 form. I had to correct it quickly."

With a final keystroke, he powered down the program, stood up, and stretched to offer his body some relief. The day's fatigue seemed to lift slightly as he moved.

Giving his wife a quick peck on the forehead, he wrapped his arm around her waist and gently guided her toward the study door.

"Did you hear what happened at the high school yesterday?" she asked with a somber tone.

"Yeah," he replied. "I could not believe it. I hope they figure out what happened. That poor girl. I did some accounting work for her father. I cannot imagine what he and his wife are going through right now."

Nearing the hall, the computer chimed. Alan paused and looked back.

"Oh no, you don't, Mr. Workaholic," his wife said, mockingly hitting his shoulder with a petite fist. "You go to the table; I'll check to see if that's Sharon's message. Then, no more computer for the night. I'm shutting it down, and I'll give you something else to do with your fingers," she winked.

He chuckled and left with a sigh, the aroma of meat and potatoes leading him on.

Downstairs, he sat surveying the pot roast, vegetables, and steamed biscuits on the cloth-covered table.

Wow, he thought, *she's going to fill me up tonight, and if I'm lucky, help me work it off later.*

He smiled, buttering his biscuit.

As he reached for the serving fork and serrated cutting knife to cut into the seasoned pot roast, Joan walked into the kitchen wearing an outlandish smile.

"I guess that was Sharon's email," he said. "What did she say? Did she send you one of her usual dirty jokes-of-the-day?" he asked while chewing the warm buttered biscuit.

"No, I read something even funnier," she replied.

Standing next to the table, she picked up a fork and knife, inspecting them as if seeing them for the first time.

After a few seconds, Alan asked, "What's with the weird smile?"

***

Alan and Joan Harbinter were married six years. No children. Middle thirties. High school sweethearts.

Police reports state they received the call at 8:33 PM. The neighbor, who made the call, reported hearing screams and suspected an intruder or a robbery.

The Harbinters were known throughout the block as a loving couple, with no evidence of domestic abuse or even minor squabbles.

The screams were audible in the background of the 911 recording as the dispatcher obtained the address from the neighbor, Mr. Alec Jennings.

The police and EMT's described the scene as one of the most horrific they had encountered in years. Mr. Harbinter's body—or what was left of it—lay sprawled out on the kitchen floor.

There were reports that he had been stabbed as many as one hundred times. The coroner I spoke with estimated it could have been closer to twice that number. The stabbing was so violent that by the fifth and fatal wound, the knife snapped after being lodged in the base of his skull.

Police surmised that once the blade broke, Joan continued with a serving fork. They found Joan leaning against the study wall near her husband's computer. She appeared lifeless, except for the shallow breaths that barely lifted her blood-soaked blouse. She was catatonic, her eyes open and seemingly lost in some private hell.

The letters 'AKL' had been carved violently into the wood-grain paneling above the computer—a message that made no sense, a code that only the deranged mind of Joan could decipher. The serving fork, its prongs twisted and stained with Alan's blood, was still in her grip, a silent witness to the horror she had unleashed.

Reporters arrived swiftly to the scene, yet the police offered scant details.

I got there just as they were loading Alan's body, draped in a crimson sheet, into the back of the ambulance.

Like the rest, I was left without answers about what had occurred in that house or what drove her to commit such a grisly act against the most devoted husband the neighborhood had ever known.

The Harbinter case dominated the news—a real shocker—but not a peep about the Sterling-Rimbaud girls from two days ago.

At Dunley's, the joint was jumping with the regulars, all bug-eyed and clutching the morning paper like a lifeline. I mentioned to the gentleman next to me how shocking it was and tried to draw parallels with the tragedy of the two girls, but all I got was an odd and confused look as if I were speaking Martian. Guess I stepped in it again.

I quieted down and polished off the rest of my breakfast, hoping I hadn't made the statement in front of any of the victims' relatives.

As the last of the customers shuffled out, most of them grim-faced, I caught sight of Thom Jenkins at the far end of the counter, underneath the drone of the ceiling television.

Thom is a reporter for the Kensington Sun, a paper from the next county over. Our paths crossed a time or two; we even shared a cold one years ago before I decided to take the big leap out this way. The guy's fanatical about facts, so much so that I slapped him with the moniker 'Egbert,' tipping my hat to the legendary Edward R. Murrow. He always had that rough-around-the-edges vibe, like a guy who's seen too much too soon.

'Hey, Thom!' I said in a forced jovial voice as I sidled up to him, lukewarm coffee cup in hand.

He looked up, and there it was—exhaustion etched deep in his mug, like he hadn't slept in weeks. The grunge that once clung to him had given way to a haggard, defeated look. His face was as jaundiced as the dog-eared notepad sprawled out in front of him.

"Hey," he rasped in a voice as dry as the Prohibition, "long time, no

see." He extended a pale, thin hand
for me to shake.

I shook it, my grip firm, like a
handshake sealed in a smoky backroom
deal. "What brings you out here?"

He let go and smoothed out the
crinkled page of the pad, slowly.
"Checking out the incidents you had
here in the last few days," he
whispered, his eyes darting back and
forth like a lookout for the mob.

"Tragic, isn't it? They say bad
news comes in threes. I hope today is
a slow news day," I said, with a laugh
as empty as a speakeasy after a raid.
"I can't believe I said that."

His eyes widened like a deer
caught in headlights. He didn't say

anything for a few seconds, as if carefully calculating his words. "It won't be. Not here, anyway. Maybe the next town."

He gave me the once-over, sizing me up. "What do you mean?" I pressed.

He glanced down at his notepad and was about to say something when the tired-looking girl behind the counter came up to ask if he needed a refill. He shooed her off with a trembling hand and looked back at me. "Got time to talk this morning? But not here."

"Sure, where do you want to go?"

"The Joshington Library. Youth section on the lower floor," he coughed.

I eyed him, curiosity piqued, as he weakly rose from his stool.

He scooped up his notepad, tossed a couple of bills on the counter and slipped past me. "Youth section's quiet—no computers. Kill your phone before we head down," he whispered, his voice disappearing into the morning hustle like fog over the Chicago River.

Aside from the two librarians— one shelving beat-up nursery rhyme books and the other bored at the checkout counter—there was a mother quietly arguing with her five- year-old, who was yanking books off the low shelves and letting them crash to the floor. The scene was chaotic, a silent battleground of wills.

Thom and I were at a small table in the back near the Young Adult section, the shadows our only companions. I felt awkward, catching glances from the bored librarian, who probably thought it was odd for two grown men to be hanging out here with no kids in tow. We probably looked like a couple of creepers.

Thom didn't seem to share my awkwardness. His face showed a tinge of relief, a rare crack in his stoic facade. I figured it was because he finally had someone to spill the beans to about the events and stories he was following—he was always a loner, from what I remember—but I think he was just glad to be away from the crowded shop. The library, with its hushed whispers and dusty corners, was a bit of a sanctuary, a place where Thom could let his guard down, if only for a moment.

I asked, "So, what did you mean about it not happening again here? That it will happen in the next town?"

"Did you hear about those suicides in Japan a few years ago?"

"What ones? There are so many nowadays," I said with a tinge of apathy.

Then it clicked. "Wait. Yeah, those twenty-seven students at that university. Can't remember the name. A fellow reporter in Chicago's brother—Kyami Yamamoto—went there. Tragic. I forget the details."

Thom flipped through the thick pad with a twitching hand.

"March 15th at 2:15 am, twenty-seven students, fifteen males, gathered at the Takatsu River.

In succession, they slit their own throats and fell into the water. No suicide notes. Just silence.

All of them were bright, gifted students in language and communication.

The students had just completed a groundbreaking project in linguistic technology.

They developed a method to decipher everything from ancient hieroglyphics to data encryption. There was even talk about Sumerian symbols and cave drawings. Their invention was set to revolutionize everything, shedding new light on the past and the future."

"So, what does that have to do with the tragedies that happened here?"

"More than you realize," he said with a raspy cough. "I uncovered the pattern months ago. Each town, each step, I've been closing in. I believe I've pinpointed the focal point where it all converges. I nearly arrived before the messages reached those poor girls. I must get to the next location before the memory fades." His hands trembled as he flipped through the pages, scanning them with an intensity that made it seem like I wasn't even there.

"Thom, what are you talking about? What pattern? What messages? You are not making sense."

He sighed and sat back in the little chair, oblivious to the looks from the dame in the corner, her kid now content with a battered Thomas the Tank book in the middle of the aisle.

"I have been following and tracking events like this since February 11th of last year, in Wheat Ridge, Colorado," he said, a tear forming in his tired eye. "I never even knew about Japan. I was so caught up in my own things. To top it off the shitty paper I worked for fired me three months ago.

Just trying to figure this out has been the only thing keeping me going. I have been tying it all together this year. How it all connects."

I looked at him, partly worried and partly embarrassed, sitting in a kiddy chair like a giant in a dollhouse. "Thom, c'mon... what's all this about? What happened in February?"

He looked at me with a dead stare, and gulped, as if summoning the courage to speak. "It was when my niece got the message. She killed the seven-year-old boy she was babysitting, then offed herself."

14 MONTHS EARLIER...

"Laurie!! C'monnnnnn! SpongeBob is supposed to be on," the brown-haired boy said through a mouthful of soggy Cheerios, his eyes wide with excitement.

"In a minute, Davy. I just want to see this for a few seconds. My uncle's a newsman, and he's going to be on TV this morning. It'll only take a second," Laurie said, cranking up the volume with one hand and taking a big bite of toast with the other.

They sat at the kitchen table, the morning sun slicing through the frosted window. "Fine," he grumbled, leaning his tired head on his hand, frowning as another spoonful of cereal splashed milk onto his pyjama top.

"See, there he is. He's the one on the left, talking to that congressman who did those bad things. My uncle's gonna be famous someday," she said with a grin, pointing at the screen.

"That's nice," Davy said, still frowning.

Laurie turned to the boy with a sympathetic look. Smirking, she switched the channel to SpongeBob. "There you go, you little monster. See, it just started," she said as his eyes lit up and she ruffled his hair.

He looked at her and giggled. "I'm not a little monster. I'm gonna be the Hulk someday!" he said with a big, goofy grin, his voice full of enthusiasm.

Ruffling his hair some more, she replied, "Not if you keep taking off your coat at the park. You still have a slight fever. You're lucky I was off school today so your mom could call me to take care of you. After SpongeBob, it's right back to bed."

"Okie dokie!" he muttered, turning back to the TV on the far end of the kitchen counter and filling his mouth with another spoonful of cereal.

Laurie leaned over and reached under the table for her backpack. She hefted it onto the table, unzipped it, and took out her laptop.

"What's that for?" Davy asked, his curiosity piqued.

"Well, since I'm stuck with the 'mini-Hulk' today," she winked at him as he giggled, "I figure I'll take this time to work on my journalism assignment." She turned it on and waited for it to start up.

"You WANT to do homework? Yuck!" he exclaimed, making a funny face.

"Hey, kiddo, even Bruce Banner had to study hard to become a scientist. How do you think 'The Hulk' was born?" Davy looked confused. "Never mind," she sighed. "Watch SpongeBob, then back to bed. Your mom's rules."

Davy groaned, "Okayyyyyyyyy…" His eyes stayed glued to the glowing television until he heard, "You've got mail," from the laptop on the kitchen table.

The screen was turned away from him, but he saw Laurie's face illuminated by the bright light. Her eyes widened as she read the message, a shadow of concern crossing her features.

What could it be? Davy wondered, feeling a chill run down his spine.

"Is that from your teacher?" he asked.

***

Needless to say, when he uttered those words, any qualms I felt about being in that library were quickly forgotten. I was totally oblivious of my surroundings as he started whispering events and times, haphazardly flipping through the notes on his pad like he was reading off a hit list.

"Keio University, Japan. The starting point. January 5th, 2012. That's when the students first documented the breakthrough. Their suicides on March 15th. A few scattered instances in China and Korea, but those are mostly conjecture." He flipped a few more pages.

"The pattern started showing in the United States on November 7th, 2012, in Lakeport, California. A father and son. Then in Lovelock, Nevada, December 26th. Two sisters. Onto Logan, Utah, January 19th, 2013. A teacher and student in a full classroom. My... my niece in Wheat Ridge following that. Moving onto Topeka, Kansas. Two twelve-year-old boys. That was on April 20th." He turned to a page with a drawn map of the United States and showed it to me.

As I looked at the tattered pages and nearly undecipherable writing, my thoughts were on his mental well-being.

I had heard about instances, mostly in people who have lost a loved one, who have been known to go to extremes in finding an explanation for the tragic events.

I felt sadness for my friend, more so than most, knowing how he used to be a strong, well-adjusted individual.

After an hour of him recounting events and dates, I became aware of more strange looks from the librarians, and I urged him to take our conversation elsewhere.

He agreed we should go to a diner at the edge of town, an old facility I had been to a few times that would have been known in the day as a 'greasy spoon' joint.

We sat in a booth near one of the large windows; the grease-caked glass giving the early afternoon an opaque quality that added to the atmosphere inside the diner.

The few patrons along the counter gave no notice to us.

The television suspended from the ceiling in the corner was tuned to some monotonous soap opera that none of the clientele was even paying attention to.

After the bored waitress poured us cups of coffee and left, he asked me in a tired voice, "Do you believe that words have power?"

"Thom, we are both journalists. You know as well as I do the power of words. What we say and how we say them is what gives us our paychecks. Not big paychecks, mind you, but it keeps food on the table," I replied, sipping my coffee, grimacing at its bitterness.

"No, no. I know that. I mean REAL power. The power to cause events or even... even call things forth?"

I cocked my head. "You mean like hocus pocus, Harry Potter stuff?" I tried not to chuckle or make any attempt to ridicule him. I felt that if

I could just humor him in some way, I might get more of a logical explanation of everything he had told me.

He paused and scanned the diner, then looked into my eyes. "Have you ever heard of the Aklo language?"

I shook my head.

He flipped to the back of the notepad. "It was first mentioned, fictionally, in 1899 by Arthur Machen, in a story he wrote called 'The White People'. H.P. Lovecraft used the reference a few times in his stories, and other authors through the years—mostly horror and Weird Tales types—have included or incorporated it in their works. It is said to have magical powers and has been known to cause death and destruction to anyone using that language to call forth..." He flipped a few pages. "...call forth 'evil and has been known to reveal knowledge to drive humans bonkers'."

"So, what you are saying is that all this is happening because of some language people are learning?"

His eyes bulged. "No... no... not learning. Being communicated or transmitted to them through digital or electronic means."

I leaned back in the booth at Lou's Diner and sighed. "Thom, how could that be? Why would someone, anyone do that? Is it some form of terrorism? If that is the case, why so random? You'd think they'd target politicians, not random nobodies in towns across the U.S. What's the point? If this has been going on, like you said, why haven't any foreign groups taken credit for it?"

"No, not random, by any means. Look at the events and how they are playing out. They are almost going in a straight line. It is a trail. Each state had one occurrence. Here, in Illinois, you have two. My theory is that there will be two or more in other states as it gets closer to where it is going."

My annoyance was starting to build; I sensed Thom noticed it, too. "Where is what going?" I said, waving my hands in the air.

"The thing that will bring about the End of Times," he whispered, his gaze unblinking.

I won't lie, a chill ran down my spine. Something was off, and I considered more about his mental well-being considering his niece's tragedy.

I hesitated, but then my journalist instinct kicked in. Rely on facts.

I thought talking reporter to reporter would bring more clarity to what Thom was telling me.

"Ok, if that is the case, I don't remember anything from Catholic school about a language called Aklo. What religion has that incorporated into their doctrine or teachings? What basis do you have that this Aklo is what is causing this? And what brought it on after all these years?"

"It is not in any Christian dogma, or any Bible, be it Quran, Mormon, Orthodox, or whatever. There are only a handful of books through time that mention Aklo: 'The Necronomicon' by Abdul Alhazred, 'The Unaussprechlichen Kulten' of von Junzt, 'De Vermis Mysteriis' by Prinn, and a few others that I cannot recall now. As for who started this, it's a mystery. There are people—worshippers, mind you—who are waiting for the right moment to set things in motion. 'When The Stars Are Right,' I read somewhere."

He could see my confusion as he continued.

He sighed and leaned over the booth, his voice dropping to a whisper. "It is bonkers, I know, but what if someone or something figured out how to use that language to 'open the door' to all this?"

Thom's eyes darted around the dimly lit diner, as if expecting shadows to come alive.

"Imagine, a language so ancient and powerful, it could summon forces beyond our comprehension."

"Ok, let's say someone did, why not just send this Aklo to everyone all at once, one quick apocalypse? Why this 'trail'?"

He flipped a page and read. "Of all those students in Japan, only one was American. From Massachusetts by the name of Keziah Upton. She was there on a scholarship. Her GPA was through the roof.

SHE was the one that suggested the Aklo texts. There were rumors around the university that her conversations with other students were awkward, to say the least. A few of the faculty had complaints that she was like a 'cult leader'.

The upper staff and others basically turned their heads because she came from a family with a lot of dough.

You and I both know the almighty dollar can be the duct tape of the masses."

I nodded my assent, remembering the politics of the big city.

"My theory, for what it is worth, is what if this 'force' was called up by her in Japan. Imagine she realized it was too big for her to handle, her and her little science-nerd cultists sacrificed themselves or something, and it is somehow 'fishing' its way back to her hometown. Maybe the 'doorway' they opened was not big enough and 'it' is using these messages as tiny bits of sacrifice to make its way."

"Thom, do you realize...I mean..." I muttered, at a loss for what else to say.

"Yes, I know. It is totally bonkers. Just hear me out. Have you run into anyone not talking about what happened here, besides the news? Anyone today about what happened in the last few days?"

I considered the guy at the donut shop. The look he gave me when I mentioned the two teenage girls the day before: his confused expression.

"Well, no. What does that have to do with anything?"

His eyes showed reluctance. "Aside from what happened in Japan, no one remembers these events I told you about. I don't even recall any of this happening. All I have to go on is documented evidence, when I interviewed everyone that was involved in any of these occurrences. They have no recollection of anything like this happening. In a few days, no one in this town will remember Rimbaud, Sterling, or the Harbinters."

"So, it is 'erasing' the thoughts of the American public so it can go on its merry way, is that what you are telling me?"

He sighed loudly. "I don't know. Maybe society nowadays is so desensitized that they don't even care. There are school shootings almost weekly now, beheadings in the Middle East. Maybe that's why it's happening now. It's 'hiding in plain sight,' as it were. Twenty years ago, if this shit happened, people would remember it for months. Now, it's just another thing we report until tomorrow." He leaned back into the seat and looked to the side, defeated.

"Thom, so what are you planning on doing? Report this to the authorities? I am having trouble believing this. With all the unexplained incidents of violence happening in the world every minute that we speak, how could just a handful of them be connected into some sort of Grand Apocalypse? It just does not make sense."

He was still looking to the side, his haggard face showing nothing. "Blind Chaos."

"What?"

"That is what the god Azathoth is—the Blind Idiot God. He blindly makes his way to where it all started and will end. He has the power to 'blind' us to our memories of him over time. He grows stronger as he gets closer, like a whirlpool. As it spins more and more, heading to the center, it gains power and momentum, and then it finally reaches the center. Straight down to the center of nothingness—the total abyss."

I looked at Thom, utterly at a loss. He needed professional help, no doubt about it. In my line of work, you run into a lot of conspiracy theorists—everyone's got something to say, especially to a journalist. But seeing someone like Thom, with his stature and work ethic, fall into this abyss? It was a gut punch. My heart sank. I'd seen it happen to a few in our field, but never thought it would happen to him. I was surprised and saddened.

I laid it all out for him, hoping to spark some clarity, but he wouldn't listen.

He argued feverishly, rattling off his so-called facts. The more he saw the doubt etched on my face, the more desperate he became. In the end, he knew he had no hope of ever convincing me.

He haggardly got out of the booth, notepad in hand, and stood there for a moment, silently studying me.

"Wait a few days. I feel it. Something's coming. I'm gonna go east. Maybe Ohio. I have a friend with a station in Columbus. He knows more about this town in Massachusetts where Upton came from. Maybe he can help me figure out my next step."

He coughed again and turned away, heading towards the diner door. The late afternoon light cast a strange silhouette on his thin form as he walked with a tired gait.

"Thom!" I shouted as he opened the door and left to the jingling of the rusty bell overhead. I knew I had failed to convince him. Desperate, I called out, "Thom. C'mon. You never told me what town Upton came from. Maybe I can see what I can do!" I scrambled out of the booth and followed.

I saw him reach his car and open the door. Just as he was about to get in, he turned and looked at me, his eyes hollow.

He shouted one word.

The breeze picked up, promising a cool night ahead, and seemed to almost swallow his word.

Thom swallowed hard, his face etched with a haunted look, then got in his car and drove away before I could reach him.

That was the last word I ever heard him say.

"Arkham."

***

The next few days were a blur of phone calls and dead ends. I tried to get in touch with The Kensington Sun about Thom. Their secretary told me he had been let go a few months back but couldn't say why. HR was no help either, as expected. I tried digging into news stations in Ohio but didn't know where to start.

Meanwhile, I was swamped with local stories: a three-alarm fire at a nursing home that claimed four lives, a rally protesting marriage equality, and a few domestic violence cases.

I wouldn't have typed this out
if it hadn't been for an article I
stumbled upon the other day.

I found the newspaper on a
bench inside the train station near my
home. I was impatiently waiting to buy
a ticket to Springfield for a
journalists' convention.

The older woman in front of me
was arguing with the cashier about
the price of a ticket when I glanced
down at the worn bench and saw it.

It was a copy of The Columbus
Dispatch from the previous day.

The headline was about an
officer killed in the line of duty, but
what caught my eye was the article
right below it, in the left-hand corner:

Reporters Killed in Murder-
Suicide Still a Mystery

COLUMBUS, OH'H Ohio police
are still investigating the
murder of Jason Halding. Mr.
Halding was a reporter for
WBNS-10 TV in Columbus for
over eight years. The motive
behind his murder by Thomas
Jenkins, whose body was found
at the scene, remains unclear at
this time.

Eyewitnesses reported seeing
the two leave Kelly's Tavern on
112th & Main at approximately
8 P.M. Their bodies were
discovered at 11:14 P.M. at Mr.
Halding's apartment on 103rd &
Milway Avenue, aS er the
landlord heard screams and
shouts from the ψoor above. The
gruesome scene was described
by an oф cer as...

My blood ran cold, and all thoughts about the ticket or the convention vanished as I bolted out of the station, not even bothering to grab the newspaper. I didn't want to read what was continued on the next page.

I stumbled to my car and vomited, my mind a whirlwind of visions. Memories that quickly faded, their lingering absence more terrifying than the clarity of the worst horror ever revealed to the human eye.

***

Sitting here at my typewriter, I'm terrified and desperate.

It's an old Electra 120 Smith & Corona, my father got me when I graduated high school, many years ago. A big, ugly beige monster that has seen better years.

      In a bid to survive, I disconnected my computer and haven't watched television in weeks. My cell phone battery is dead, and I stopped the service plan last month. I keep it on top of the pile of reports, articles, and such, as a reminder.

      I even had my landline reconnected.

      It's amazingly difficult to try and purchase a landline nowadays. They're going the way of the dodo bird. I feel that pretty soon, mankind will join that long-lost creature.

      That night after leaving the train station, I wrote down everything

I could remember about the conversations Thom and I had.

It took me months to locate the events he told me about.

I left them all out on the small kitchen countertop for my tired eyes to see in the morning. There were a few mornings that I looked at those papers with confusion, but the more I read through them each day, the more it stayed at the forefront of my mind.

There are snatches sometimes of events and memories in my head that blow away like the smoke from an extinguished candle flame.

I tried following up on the events that happened in my town, but everywhere I went seemed to finish in a dead end.

There was one time I went to the school Jessica and Sara attended, to ask about them, but the records department had no listing. I tried to talk to other faculty, but the suspicious teachers made me realize I wouldn't get anywhere. I did run into a student who tried to stop Jessica that day, but when I questioned him, he gave me a queer look and just shook his head.

I went to the donut shop this morning after not going there for a while. I looked at the tired, half-awake faces of the patrons and I almost had a feeling of déjà vu from that day I encountered Thom.

It was kind of surreal seeing the empty spot near the counter under the television as it blared the morning news. It was almost like his spot was purposely abandoned.

Looking up at the screen, I saw the newscast about a string of murder-suicides in a town in Massachusetts. The screen showed footage of a cordoned-off set of concrete stairs in front of a university. It seemed that it happened in a classroom that morning, and how many students and teachers were involved had yet to be determined.

I didn't stay to listen to the rest of the broadcast.

When they said the town's name, I knew the blind idiot force had finally reached its destination.

As I looked at the customers, oblivious to the newscast on the screen, I also knew that God had the power to blind others.

I left and got into my car. The air was thick with the hum inside that shop, a sound that brought a chill to my bones.

The sound of different cell phone tones all going off simultaneously.

As I drove through the dimly lit streets, the ringing phones echoed in my mind. Each tone a fatal shot. The force had reached everyone at once, amplifying the dread in my chest.

Sitting here in the dark, I'm terrified. I know what is to come. I hear the screams and sounds of violence in the other apartments around me. Some sirens wail in the distance, but none are near me.

I am hoping someone will find these pages I type. It is hard for me to remember why I am typing this as I go on.

The shrieks and cries from the other tenants seem to fade, leaving me in an eerie silence except for my phone glowing and vibrating.

Didn't I just type about the battery being dead? Maybe if I keep typing, it will distract me from picking it up. I have to keep typing something, keep my hand away. I have to—

ABOUT THE AUTHOR

Rick Powell

Rick Powell is a resident of Oak Forest, Illinois, U.S.A. Rick began writing horror and dark fiction in 2012. His poetic and narrative talents have graced the pages of various publications, including Infernal Ink Magazine and the tantalizing anthology Lustcraftian Horrors: Erotic Stories Inspired by H.P. Lovecraft.

ABOUT THE EDITORS

Joseph Mykut

Joseph Mykut is a native of Alabama. They are an author, artist, illustrator, editor, photographer, and agent. Their artwork and photography are on display internationally in

Ontario, Canada and can be found in the anthologies *3 Amigos Ink and Splatter Lonely Soul in the Darkness*, *The Way of the Crow and Shattered Psyche*. All anthologies are **I Ain't Your Marionette Press** publications out of Canada. They also authored and illustrated the children's book, "Beautiful Boy", of the same publishing house.

Joseph's art and photography uniquely focuses on the random, seemingly unimportant aspects of the everyday environment surrounding us. They hope this draws attention to the deeper details that express the magic and beauty in the otherwise mundane.

As a member of the LGBTQ2+ community as well as walking the path of Shamanism, they hope to create and represent a more tangible bridge between the physical life experience and the world beyond our physical senses.

Joseph was born and raised in the deep south of the United Sates in what's known as the bible belt. His influences have developed over time to be more of the universe and of spirituality rather than religion.

However, Joseph is an ordained minister with the Universal Life Church as it aligns with his perspective that there is truth found in all religious beliefs as they are all smaller pieces to a greater picture.

They identify as a two spirited being or even multi spirited being and identify with all ideas of the gender spectrum. They believe in the existence of both light and dark or positive and negative energies leaving the truth of who we are to be found in the balance of those energies

Marie Moldovan

Marie Moldovan is a Saskatchewan native and Ontario immigrant. Some would call them a reverse snowbird, who feels most comfortable surrounded by snowcapped mountains.

Nomadic by nature, Marie is multifaceted and has mastered many skills. They dub themselves a jack of many trades and master of some. However, because Marie has acquired a plethora of diplomas spanning the educational spectrum, Marie's mother on the contrary would call them a professional student.

Marie would accredit their adaptability to the training they received as a Canadian Forces medic, and their artistic ability to their family. Both attributes have aided her along their journey from the points of homelessness and despair to the place of stability and optimism Marie has arrived at today.

In 2018, Marie was diagnosed with service-related PTSD, and within the same breath of time became a widow.

Unresolved trauma, and the loss of their husband caused Marie to skirt the edges of insanity. Faced with losing complete touch with reality, they returned to writing and art.

In a sense writing and art saved Marie's life, at least that's their claim. Fortunately, for the world, Marie's choice to embrace creation has led them to captain a new life as a publisher, illustrator, writer and artist.

Marie is the author of **20 years of Winter, *Miss Sally Anne*** and has currently opened the doors of her own publication organization, aptly named, **I Ain't Your Marionette Press**.

20 Years of Winter is an autobiographical collection of poetry and art. She published it in hopes to make a way for others who have suffered similar traumas to feel safe knowing that they are not alone nor are they to blame for their experiences. *20 Years of Winter* is Marie's source of empowerment offered to those victims to stand up to their perpetrators and to speak out against victim shaming.

ABOUT THE PUBLISHER

Alas, who are we, marionettes on strings? And what do we stand for, puppeteers of our destiny?

I Ain't Your Marionette distinguishes itself as a stronghold of artistic liberation. At its helm, Marie Moldovan, once a marionette of circumstance, now orchestrates a symphony of narrative freedom. The company's sanctuary breathes life into marionette authors, whose tales of resilience and aspiration paint a vivid tableau of human spirit.

The press's hallmark anthologies, **Shattered Psyche** and **The Way of The Crow**, are more than mere collections; they are immersive experiences that beckon readers to venture beyond the mundane. Each story or visual masterpiece is a declaration of independence, a narrative that defies the norm and invites a reimagining of the world.

The **Voces Animarum** exhibition, alongside the **Shattered Psyche Traveling Showcase** and **Colours of Collaboration**, exemplifies the press's dedication to breaking new ground in literary and artistic expression. These ventures not only elevate the company's stature but also reverberate through the artistic community, transforming subdued creative murmurs into a powerful chorus that resonates far and wide.

FURTHER READING

***

Dive deeper into the captivating worlds crafted by Rick Powell. Each story in this collection explores the boundaries of love, loss, and the supernatural, inviting readers to confront their deepest fears and desires. Whether you're drawn to tales of obsession, apocalyptic nightmares, or chilling mysteries, there's something here for every lover of dark fiction.

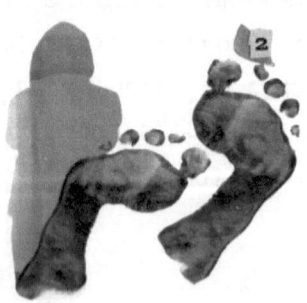

Two Lost Souls:

Love, like life, is one of the oldest mysteries. But what happens when love turns into an obsession? When the boundaries between passion and madness blur, and the veil between the supernatural and natural world is cast aside? David believed his bond with his wife Helen was unbreakable, forged in the fires of life's trials. Yet, even the strongest love can be tested by the shadows that lurk in the corners of our hearts—and the darkness of a graveyard.

A Day of Ochre, Ascending:

In this apocalyptic nightmare inspired by Robert W. Chambers' The King in Yellow, a man's ordinary stroll with his dog turns into a nightmare. Each step plunges Walter and Archie deeper into a world of whispered doom. Will they escape, or will the nightmare consume them?

A Banquet of Panacea:

The loss of a child is a wound that never heals. But what if there was a way to move forward, a method so unthinkable it's only whispered about in the shadows? The Richards are living every parent's worst nightmare, their child's life stolen by a remorseless killer. In their darkest hour, they encounter Zhang, a billionaire with a chilling solution: when the justice system fails, he invites the families to a dinner shrouded in mystery and darkness.

Harold:

Frank is a seasoned detective with an uncanny 'feel' for things—a gift that has often guided him through the toughest cases. But this gift comes at a steep price. After years of risking his family and marriage for the job, Frank longs to slow down and reconnect with his loved ones. However, fate has other plans. A mysterious journal lands in his hands, chronicling the twisted crimes of a madman named Harold. Is this a work of fiction, or a chilling true-life account of a delusional killer?

Winston:

Julie lives with her mother in a rundown part of town, struggling to adjust to her mom's new boyfriend, a man she distrusts for many reasons. During a fateful walk home, she encounters Winston, an enigmatic old man whose presence is as captivating as it is mysterious. As their bond deepens, Julie's life begins to change in unimaginable ways. Who is Winston, and what secrets does he hold that could lift Julie out of her adversity? Is he a savior, or a messenger of doom?

Ornament:

The holidays are a time for gathering with friends, family, and loved ones. Blazing fireplaces warm the bodies and hearts of those closest to us, as we share anecdotes of the year's events while the snow and bitter cold blow outside. But for Judith, the cold seeps inside her home, reflecting the turmoil in her life with John. Lies, cheating, and psychological abuse overshadow the season's joy, leaving her without a solution in sight.

Messages:

In a world where technology races forward, leaving yesterday's marvels in the dust, what if someone dared to blend ancient secrets with modern innovations? "Messages" delves into this terrifying possibility. Follow the harrowing journey of a reporter who uncovers the story of a lifetime—a story that could very well be his last. As he digs deeper, he finds himself trapped in a web of dark forces and apocalyptic realities.

A Glimpse Beyond the Veil:

The final book, *A Glimpse Beyond the Veil*, brings together all seven stories. Within this anthology of shadows, secrets writhe through the corridors of forgotten places and sinister whispers shroud the night. Each tale lures readers into the abyss to confront their deepest fears. This collection is a haunting exploration of the human condition and beckons readers to step into a world where reality blurs with the supernatural.

Thank

you for

your

support.

www.ingramcontent.com/pod-product-compliance
Lightning Source LLC
Chambersburg PA
CBHW030539180626
46810CB00005B/1936